A bit about t

The Sheep of
have been in my   ⎯ years, but
I have been so busy in my life that it is only
now since my wonderful husband Jim passed
away and I retired that I've been able to fulfil
my lifelong ambition to finish writing them
and share them with you. I hope adults will
enjoy reading them to children, and children
will love listening and reading them, too, for
many years to come and, maybe one day you
will get the opportunity to visit the beautiful Lake District in England,
Madeira, or Iceland.

Introduction to *The Sheep of Poshington Hall Farm*

Hekla and Freya live at Poshington Hall Farm in the Lake District. They
look like many sheep with silly smiles, beautiful woollen fleeces and
horns, but they are not. They are in fact Icelandic sheep that possess
secret troll-given magical powers in their fleeces and go on wonderful
adventures. In this book, the sheep go on a cruise and use their troll-given
magic to help catch robbers.

The Sheep of Poshington Hall Farm Series

The Sheep of Poshington Hall Farm - Book 1

*The Sheep of Poshington Hall Farm's
Flying Visit to Iceland - Book 2*

*The Sheep of Poshington Hall Farm
Go on a Cruise - Book 3*

The Sheep of Poshington Hall Farm
books are dedicated to
my wonderful late husband Jim.

The Sheep

of

Poshington Hall Farm

Go On A Cruise

The day following the successful rescue of their relatives from Iceland, Hekla and Freya the Icelandic sheep were joined on the fells in England's beautiful Lake District by their nosey mischievous neighbour Malcolm the magpie.

Malcolm was very keen to hear all about the rescue and their Icelandic adventure. After all, it was Malcolm who had put the sheep in touch with his mate, Archie the Arctic tern. Archie had been the sheep's flying instructor and guide to Iceland.

"Thank you so much for your help Malcolm," Freya began, and then Hekla joined in with her three-pennyworth, "As sheep-birds we flew miles and miles, over land and sea on our journey to Iceland, guided by Archie."

"Higher and higher," added Hekla.

"Further and further," said Freya.

As usual, Malcolm was all ears at first as he listened intently to the sheep. They told him all about the Troll's parlour, and his horrid appetite for stinking fermented shark and rotting cabbage. And, how they'd carried their nieces and nephews back home in their horns using troll magic.

After a while Malcolm began to yawn, then batted his head with a wing to wake himself up. You see, when the sheep got excited, they spoke very fast and kept talking over each other, so much so, that Malcolm heard very little of their adventure.

Malcolm eventually stopped listening to the pair altogether as his thoughts turned to his tea, and what he was going to have with the tasty bird table of scraps he'd found earlier. He knew that one way to shut the sheep up was to annoy them. So, he cocked his head to one side and made some clicking noises with his beak, and they stopped.

Then in his most irritating whiny voice said, "After you left, it got me thinking that instead of flying, you could of course have taken a cruise."

The pair stared so vacantly at Malcolm that he had to explain what a cruise was, and how his gull friends would often save their wings on long journeys by hitching a lift on a passing cruise ship.

The sheep looked at each other thoughtfully.

"Oh no," said Malcom. He realised too late that he'd been just a tad too hasty. Fancy putting the idea of a cruise in the sheep's heads.

"I wish I hadn't mentioned it," he said.

"No, no, that's a brilliant idea!" Freya bleated in excitement.

"I suppose we could try one?" agreed Hekla.

The pair loved a good adventure.

After some hard thought Hekla piped up, "You know, Bouncer the sheep dog told me that Beryl the farmer's wife is planning another holiday with Farmer Joe to Iceland. Well, how about us taking a cruise at the same time? That way they'd never know we'd gone."

"What a great idea," agreed Freya.

That day Bouncer wandered over to join the sheep. He was very clever and understood a lot of what people said. So, when Hekla and Freya asked him to let them know when Beryl and Farmer Joe were taking their next holiday, he was only too happy to help.

Bouncer was intrigued when he heard the sheep's plan, then worriedly said, "What are you going to eat? They don't have fells on ships. I've seen pictures in holiday brochures."

The sheep looked at each other in a puzzled manner and decided to sleep on the problem.

In the morning, Freya came up with an idea. "If we can't find any food on the ship, we'll have to zoom off to the nearest grazing land and back."

"We can always eat seaweed from the shoreline like our cousins do in the Hebrides," suggested Hekla.

And they knew how to use their zoom magic as they'd used it when they returned from Iceland with their rescued relatives.

"We'll need to be invisible most of the time, too, even though our droppings aren't!" Freya said with a sheepish grin. The sheep giggled.

Malcolm had been busy making enquiries about cruise ships with his seagull pals. Geoffrey the black-headed gull told him that a port called Liverpool, not too far away from them, had cruise ships leaving for all sorts of exciting destinations. But, he needed to know the exact departure date and for how long. "Time and tide wait for no man," he muttered.

A couple of days later, Bouncer bounded over to the sheep wagging his tail. He had a piece of paper in his mouth with Beryl's handwriting on it, and in big letters she'd written 'LEAVE WEDNESDAY 28 OCTOBER, BACK 11 NOVEMBER.'

"That's it and it's a Wednesday, our favourite day!" Freya squealed with delight and summoned Malcolm, who arrived in a whooshing flapping flash. With just two clicks and a strange whistle, Malcolm signalled to Geoffrey the gull who landed nearby.

The sheep briefed Geoffrey and thanked Bouncer who ran off very pleased with himself, wagging his tail even more.

"What've you got there, boy?" Farmer Joe said and looked at the chewed-up damp bit of paper.

Later that evening he discussed Beryl's plans with her over a large supper bowl of pasta smothered in rich tomato sauce and a mug of hot tea.

Geoffrey went off to check out the cruise ships that matched Beryl's dates. The next day he came whooshing back.

"Where are we going?" the sheep squealed together in excitement.

"Somewhere called Portugal and Madeira," squawked Geoffrey.

He then gave them a brief description of the places, especially the tropical plants. It all sounded very exotic.

"The weather will be warm in Madeira and not too bad in Portugal," Geoffrey explained.

"We should be fine," said the sheep. They both knew they could always cool themselves down with magic.

The sheep had kept their sunglasses and scarves they'd used to disguise themselves on their previous adventure as visitors to Poshington Hall. They thought that they might come in handy for the cruise.

On the night of the 27th October, Hekla and Freya licked their fleeces and said the magic words, "Galdur galdur make us only visible when we say, O great troll." Then they practised their invisibility a few times with

"Galdur on" and "Galdur off". Once they were happy that their magic worked, they then used it to practise flying again. It worked.

Geoffrey arrived early on 28th October and gave the sheep directions for the Liverpool cruise terminal.

The sheep watched Beryl, Farmer Joe, and their daughter Jenny say their goodbyes to Jim the farm labourer. Jim was now in charge of the farm while they were away. Soon their taxi arrived. It took a while to load all their suitcases in the boot, but once they were all in, they waved goodbye to Jim and Bouncer.

The sheep waited until the taxi had disappeared down the lane, then used their zoom magic to leave. The sheep bounced up and down and the more they bounced the higher they flew.

"Goodbye!" shouted Malcolm.

"Have a safe trip," bleated the flock.

Mr Boohoo the scarecrow looked up from the field and waved them off.

Geoffrey the seagull went with them as their guide for the first few miles. "Good luck!" he cried as he left them on the right flight path for Liverpool.

The ship they had to catch was called the 'Queen Gloriana' and it was waiting for them, moored on the quayside. It looked very grand with a bright red bottom-half and a very regal looking figurehead of a Queen on its bow.

Quickly they used their invisibility magic to land on the top deck. They mooched around until they found a nice comfy white bench to sit down on. The bench had a lovely royal blue plump wipeable cushioned seat, and from there they had a marvellous birds-eye view over the quayside. The quayside was very busy and packed with smiling families, excited children, middle-aged squabbling anxious aunts, and elderly people preparing to board the ship.

"I wonder where the human flock will all sleep?" Freya mused.

From the loudspeaker announcements the sheep quickly learned that all the people not in a uniform were called passengers, and those wearing uniforms were known as crew.

Freya and Hekla decided to have their photos taken as they'd seen the queue of passengers having theirs done.

It seemed ages before all the passenger flock were boarded and had had their embarkation photos taken. Then, just as the last couple were snapped, the people taking photos put their cameras down and chatted.

In a moment the sheep had bounced to the bottom of the boarding gangway landing with a 'boing'.

Next, they briefly removed their invisibility, quickly put on their scarves and sunglasses, then picked up the camera and began taking photos of each other. It was such fun. Instead of saying "cheese" they said "thistles" to achieve the perfect false smile. But, they didn't really have to try too hard because they were actually very happy and extremely excited.

The photographers saw the flashes and scratched their heads. But, by the time they'd noticed anything unusual the sheep were invisible again.

Although the sheep could fly, they used the stairs to get up to the decks to avoid the 'passenger lifts' which were very crowded.

The photographers went off to their studio on Deck 7 to print off the passengers' photographs in readiness for the evening display boards.

Soon the prints were run off and displayed on the racks in the 'Take your memories home corner'.

The 'corner' was very popular with the passengers. There they could look at the snaps and pick out their favourite prints. But, more importantly, for the photographers, they earned £25 for each one. The photographers giggled over some of the prints as they worked and sipped cups of coffee. There were all sorts of passengers and amongst them some very odd-looking people, along with old couples who were probably on a trip of a lifetime.

Then Johnny the Lead Photographer remarked to his assistant Sadie, "Look at these two, don't remember taking these ones, do you?" Sadie couldn't remember taking them either.

"But, hey, there's ugly and there's UGLY," said Sadie and, of course, it was Hekla and Freya.

The sheep by now were feeling hungry and so went in search of something tasty to eat. They tried a nibble of the flowers in the vases on the coffee tables in the reception lounge, but these turned out to be chewy plastic and not very nice at all.

Then on a lower deck by a door they saw a couple of men chatting. The men wore checked trousers and white hats and were smoking cigarettes outside on the deck. When they'd finished, they flicked their cigarette butts into the tall bin ashtrays then disappeared through a door. The door had a notice on it which read "Crew Only" and it looked very busy inside. So, they waited for the door to open again, and sure enough it did.

"Quick," said Hekla and the sheep slipped through the door and found themselves in a very large store room.

The place was packed with big catering sized tins, fresh produce with huge bottles of vinegar, tubs of mustard, and custard powder. There were sacks of potatoes and rice, nets of cabbages, slabs of chocolate, ginger, spices, and truckle cheeses of every description. Beyond the store they could see people in hats and aprons with blue gloves on preparing and cooking food.

They quietly tiptoed around the store room, and to their delight saw a big cardboard box with the word 'Hay' written in large black letters on the side. They had seen the word 'Hay' before on a box in the barn at the farm and knew what it meant - 'Food'.

Quickly the pair chewed through the cardboard, and sure enough inside the box they found some very yummy hay. They chomped away unnoticed until they'd completely polished the lot off!

All that hay had made the sheep thirsty, so after lunch they headed for a drink from the paddling pool. Nobody was in it, so they had a good drink and washed their feet. Of course, sheep don't wear nappies and although they were invisible, their droppings were not. The poo soon floated to the top of the pool. Next, they went to the lift lobby area on the Deck.

There weren't many passengers around as most were unpacking their suitcases in their cabins, or eating snacks on the decks in the food outlets.

Next, came the ship evacuation drill. Once all the excitement of wearing life-jackets, the drill, and swapping stories of the 'Titanic' had subsided, the ship sounded its loud horn three times, and then gently slipped anchor to begin its voyage south.

There was much cheering and waving on the decks, and the first rounds of drinks were being ordered and brought to the tables by smart waiters.

The sheep waited patiently in the lift lobby area, and when one of the lift doors opened, they decided to give it a go. The lift was already populated by two rather large ladies. However, they just about managed to squeeze themselves in, too. The sheep had no idea where they were going and couldn't reach the floor buttons on the side panel by the doors. As each floor passed the doors opened and waiting passengers looked in, smiled and politely said, "We'll wait for the next one."

The sheep left more droppings in the lift and the two ladies looked at each other concerned. When the ladies got out, the sheep did, too. More passengers got in and when some of them smelt the poo in the lift, they pinched their noses and quickly got out saying, "We'll walk." Before long, the lift had an 'out of order' sign slapped on the door and a man with a mop and bucket was cleaning the floor.

The sheep went back to the paddling pool via the stairs, this time for another drink, but found a red and white tape rope around it and a notice that read "Pool closed for hygienic reasons". The sheep had no idea what that meant. So, in case it was bad they decided to drink from the jacuzzi pool instead.

The jacuzzi water was warm and when they turned to go Hekla left another dropping in the pool.

The invisible sheep sat in deck chairs and watched passengers come and go. They then saw the two large ladies they'd met in the lift arrive at the jacuzzi dressed in large colourful bathing costumes. Fascinated, the sheep watched as the ladies carefully lowered themselves into the jacuzzi clutching large Pina Colada cocktails decorated with straws, umbrellas, swizzle sticks, slices of oranges and cherries.

When the bubbles in the jacuzzi stopped they were just about to press the 'restart' button on the side when one of them noticed a poo floating on the surface.

"Hilda!" Mavis exclaimed in horror as she pointed out the poo.

Quickly they got out and went to report the issue to Amy the Guest Relations Manager. Amy thanked them for bringing it to her attention, but was not that shocked, as she'd seen this kind of thing before and immediately radioed for a 'cleaning operative' on her Walkie-talkie. Amy looked cross.

"It wasn't us," said Mavis and Hilda as they walked off. Soon another red and white tape rope ran around the jacuzzi with the same sign as the paddling pool.

By now passengers had begun to line up at reception on deck 5 to complain about facilities being out of order.

Later that evening during the Captain's 'welcome' announcement, he mentioned the importance of hygiene on board. He talked about washing and sanitising hands after using the loos and before eating in the dining rooms. Then in a concerned voice he asked parents and guardians of little-ones to ensure they wore waterproof nappies in pools and, that under no circumstances were they to be allowed in the jacuzzi pools for 'safety reasons'.

The poshest of poshest of all the on-board restaurants was 'The Royal Gloriana'. The menu was displayed outside its main entrance on the wall in a gilded glass case. And, for that evening showed the celebrity chef menu special as 'Smoked lamb in hay'. The restaurant tables were booked out quickly, as passengers liked the look of the posh nosh menu, especially the lamb. Many passengers had seen smoked lamb being prepared on TV cooking programmes, and it was something to try and then boast to their friends about when they got home. The celebrity Head Chef called for the lamb to be brought up to the diners who had booked tables for the first sitting at 6 pm.

The cooks looked everywhere for the hay to go with the lamb, but the only thing they found in its place was a chewed up empty old box. And, so, with very red faces the cooks told the Head Chef that they had the lamb but no hay.

Everything had gone wrong on the opening day for the Head Chef. That morning his alarm clock had stopped working as the battery was dead, and so he'd overslept. He also had overeaten the night before and now had a tummy ache. To wake himself up he had a strong black coffee, but then in his hurry to get ready had spilt it. Then, he couldn't find a pair of matching socks and now this! It was the last straw for him and he flew into a hissy fit. First his tall white chef's hat whooshed across the kitchen, this was followed soon after by a big wooden spoon that clattered noisily to the floor. He then banged his fist on a chopping table and stamped his left foot as he shouted at the top of his voice "imbeciles" and kept repeating "Ooh la la". Swiftly the staff got well out of his way, as he continued to fume and mop his sweaty brow with a large napkin. His sous chef Claude managed eventually to calm him down. He then apologised to his staff and then personally to the diners who had ordered the lamb. He could see how disappointed they were from their miserable frowning faces. The diners were cross, especially as they had paid supplements to dine in the poshest restaurant. As compensation, every passenger who had ordered the 'Chef's special' got a voucher for a free single-scoop of vanilla, strawberry, or chocolate ice-cream with a sprinkle of their choice.

Luckily, the sheep didn't see their dead slaughtered fellow sheep because they had been too busy following

Mavis and Hilda around, and they even managed to sneak into the ladies' cabin.

The ladies had a large cabin with two enormous single beds and enough room for the sheep to hide under the beds. They also had a big bathroom, a spacious lounge, a smaller seated area, and a balcony. The sheep watched them do their droppings in the toilet and, when nobody was watching, they tried out the toilet, too. Later on, Hilda quietly mentioned the delicate matter to Mavis, "I do wish you'd flush the loo after you."

Mavis assured Hilda that she did, but maybe she was getting a bit forgetful. "Sorry, a senior moment," she said. Hilda understood as she had those, too.

As singleton friends Mavis and Hilda hoped to find two nice gentlemen companions on the cruise, ones that they could share their love of dance with, and who loved their food as much as they did. They had signed up for special singles cocktail party receptions and dancing lessons. To catch gentlemen's eyes, they had brought with them the most enormous sparkling ball gowns for the evenings. To match their dresses, they had dyed their grey hair with blue and pink rinses, and they'd brought their finest gold, diamonds, and pearl jewellery to finish off their glamorous evening look.

As both of the ladies were a bit forgetful, Mavis had written the room safe code on a piece of paper which she hid in her knicker drawer.

After their early dinner sitting, the ladies decided to find their boarding photos on Deck 7. Of course, the sheep followed. Mavis and Hilda searched through all the photos.

"I think I saw your pics on the third display," said a lady behind them. They thanked the lady who introduced herself, "My name's Hazel."

The sheep looked at each other in astonishment. It was none other than Hazel the volunteer guide and ticket desk clerk from Poshington Hall.

"Crikey," whispered Hekla. They'd have to be very careful now not to be found out. (You see the sheep could see each other, but people couldn't see them, which in the circumstances was just as well!).

"There are some rather odd couples on board," Hazel remarked.

"Yes, aren't there? Take those two, for instance," Hilda said and pointed to Hekla and Freya's photos. Hazel gasped, shook a little and rubbed her eyes as if she'd seen a ghost.

"Whatever is the matter, Hazel?" said Mavis and put her arm around Hazel to comfort her. "I know they are ugly, but they aren't that bad. So, why don't you just come along with us and sit down, and we'll all have a nice cuppa."

They walked slowly to the nearby coffee shop and ordered a pot of tea for three. All Hazel kept saying was "Sh sh sh sheep".

"I know they did look a bit sheepish, but how can there be sheep on the ship?" Mavis said. Then she paused a while as she thought about the poo around. But decided it couldn't possibly be true. Hazel in her mind remained unconvinced.

Because their photos had upset Hazel so much, the sheep waited until nobody was looking and took their photos off the display board. Then they magicked the photos into tiny take-away sizes and tucked them into Hekla's horns.

After their tea they all went back again together to look at the sheep-lady photos that had upset Hazel, but they were gone.

"They must have been sold while we were having tea," said Mavis. Hazel remained sceptical.

Meanwhile, Johnny and Sadie were doing such a brisk business that it was only later that evening they realised the ugly ladies' photos were missing.

"I knew they looked a bit dodgy," said Sadie.

"Some people are just plain sad," added Johnny. However, because they had made a lot of money that day, they decided not to cause a fuss.

The next two days were spent at sea, and the sheep got to know the ship pretty well. When nobody was looking, they tried out a game of shuttle board on deck, watched the Head Chef demonstrate how to make a perfect raspberry pavlova, and played ping-pong. On their first night the pair climbed into a lifeboat and were gently rocked to sleep by the motion of the waves.

Unbeknown to the sheep and passengers there were a pair of wicked thieves on board, who had met in prison, and on leaving had decided to call themselves Charles and Ernest when they wanted to be posh. Their real names were Bill and Bert. They used money they'd stolen to buy cruise tickets hoping to find more riches on the ship. They were particularly keen to meet rich mature ladies to make friends with and then rob.

That night before the ship was due to dock at Funchal, the ship's entertainment team had organised a lively evening's event programme. It kicked off with a Mexican themed night, with the ship's band playing Mexican Music. There were enormous inflated bananas, pineapples, and spiky cacti blow-up decorations around the place. The first hour of the evening from 7 pm to 8 pm was 'Happy Hour' offering passengers 2 for the price of 1 drinks and cocktails.

So, when Mavis and Hilda arrived at 7.30 pm the bartenders were in full-swing and very busy throwing and catching cocktail shakers. The waiters wore sombreros and danced around with their trays of drinks dodging people as they went about their work. Their trays were heavy with margaritas and tequila slammers for the adults and frothy milkshakes and pop for children.

The sheep, of course, didn't drink human drinks apart from water. However, they liked the idea of eating corn. Bowls of 'corn on the cob' were put out on all the tables in the lounge along with tortilla chips and salsa dips. The first bowls of snacks were 'free' and the sheep sat at the two empty chairs unseen by the ladies on their table for four. However, every time one of the ladies went to try a piece of corn she found it had mysteriously disappeared, and thinking that the other had taken it, kept asking for more. The waiters didn't mind as extra bowls were added to their customer's room bills, and the more they sold, the bigger their bonuses would be at the end of the cruise.

The sheep watched the show. It was a real fiesta, so full of vibrant colours with swirling skirts, flapping fans, songs, and included a Mexican hat-dancer. The main show ended with the audience clapping and participating in a massive Mexican wave. Then the passengers were invited by Hugo the Entertainment Officer to join him on the stage for a spot of dancing.

The band played dance music for the Salsa, Cha Cha, Samba, and Tango. Mavis and Hilda got up from their chairs and moved onto the stage dance floor. Clasping hands they began to dance awkwardly together. Shortly after the first dance had finished, they were approached by two rather good-looking elderly gentlemen in smart dinner jackets and bow ties who asked them to dance. The ladies were flattered and they both thought 'this could be it!' Round and round the dance floor they went until they were quite dizzy and puffed out.

The sheep had also left their chairs and were having a go at dancing, too. But, they did more bumping into dancers and treading on people's toes than dancing. Because the sheep couldn't be seen, dancing partners kept blaming each other for being clumsy. Of course, sheep will be sheep and their droppings soon mounted up. Then a couple of salsa dancers slipped on the poo and skidded into the band, the lady shrieked as she twisted her ankle, and her partner just about managed to steady himself. The other dancers gawped at the unfortunate pair. The music and dancing stopped. The saxophone player adjusted his glasses which had been knocked off his nose and the drummer picked up his drumsticks. Tissues came out of handbags as the dancers checked their shoes and wiped off the poo. Hugo appeared and apologised to the dancers for their distress. Again, a cleaning operative was summoned. Hugo gave the lady who had twisted her ankle a voucher for a free 'tequila slammer' or fruit juice of her choice, then assisted her off the stage as she hobbled awkwardly to her seat clutching a pair of soiled gold slingback sandals. Once she had sat down she ordered the 'free' tequila slammer followed by a double brandy to calm her nerves. By now Amy the Customer Relations Manager from Reception was pretty convinced she knew who the culprits were, but couldn't say for sure. The sheep went back to their chairs and decided just to watch.

The dancers went back to their seats, too, while the cleaning took place, and, the gentlemen escorted the ladies back to their table and asked if they could join them.

"Of course you may," said Mavis.

"We'd be delighted," said Hilda and gestured to the men to sit down.

Quickly, the sheep jumped off their chairs and found two more unoccupied ones nearby along with untouched 'free bowls' of corn. Delighted with more food, they munched away. The gentlemen ordered drinks for the table. Mavis was drinking Snowball cocktails by the gallon with lots of cherries, and Hilda was gulping down copious quantities of Vodka Martinis. The gentlemen, not realising it, had sat straight down on some of the sheep droppings. Shortly after they had sat down dancing started again, but the four of them and sheep decided to remain seated.

The gentlemen introduced themselves as Charles and Ernest and then Hilda asked them what they did for a living. Charles told them that the pair hadn't worked for years. Of course it was true, but they didn't tell them the real reason for not working was due to them spending rather a lot of time in prison.

"We've got loads of money and enjoy spending it on life's little luxuries," Ernest boasted.

"We like our cars and are especially keen on luxury models. I have a vintage Bentley. Perhaps you might like to come for a spin in it sometime?" Charles boasted.

"No, I am sure the ladies would prefer coming out in my snazzy Lamborghini," Ernest joked.

Mavis then asked them about their hobbies and they both said that they enjoyed playing golf, dancing, and eating in fancy restaurants.

"We tend to use cruises to drop into our houses scattered around the world near golf courses, where we play and stay," explained Charles. They then began their 'charm offensive'.

"You two are very beautiful and such marvellous dancers," commented Ernest, and of course Charles agreed. The ladies were foolishly flattered, and the bigger the lies the more their mouths dropped in amazement, and they kept saying "gosh!" and "really". The gentlemen found out the ladies' cabin number from their cruise pass they'd carelessly put on the table.

Then Hilda asked the men if they would be joining them for bingo the following afternoon. Unfortunately, the men said that they would still be doing an excursion at 4 pm and were unable to join them, but suggested dancing again at 8 pm.

Mavis and Hilda told the gentlemen that they were doing an early morning excursion once the ship had docked at Funchal on the beautiful island of Madeira.

Mavis added, "Our excursion takes us to the botanical gardens and we're going on a wine tasting, too, at an old Madeira wine vault. And, before we return to the ship, we are taking an optional toboggan ride from the top of a hill by the gardens."

Charles then confessed that their excursion actually amounted to a round of golf. The ladies laughed.

After all the chatting, drinking, and dancing, the gentlemen escorted their dancing partners back to their cabin and said, "Goodnight."

Both were a little tipsy. Mavis had been fiddling nervously with her earrings on their way back to the cabin, and accidentally dropped one of them on the floor in the corridor outside. She only realised her earring was missing when she went to put her jewellery away in the safe for the night. So, she decided to go out and look for it. But, just as she was about to open their cabin door there was a knock. It was Ernest, "I believe this is yours," he said and opened his hand. There was her earring.

"Thank you so much," gushed Mavis. "I'll just put it away with the other one," she said, but as she took it, she let the paper with the safe code drop to the floor; at once Ernest noted the code.

"Well goodnight again, ladies," he said and left.

"How kind of Ernest to take the trouble to bring my earring back, even though I thought he whiffed a bit," remarked Mavis. Hilda had smelt the nasty smell too, and although she enjoyed the dancing, the smell had put her off the men.

The sheep were quickly through the open cabin door and were following Ernest along the corridor to the cabin he shared with Charles. The sheep sneaked inside. It was a lot smaller than the ladies' cabin, and didn't have a window, but still there was room under the single beds to hide and sleep if they down-sized themselves with their fleece magic.

"I've got it," said Bert excitedly and wrote down the code before he forgot it on a piece of complimentary 'Queen Gloriana' notepaper.

Bill knew exactly what it was. "Great!" he exclaimed.

Carefully they removed their grey wigs and peeled off their false moustaches and eyebrows, brushed their teeth, and were just about to hang their suits up in the closet when they noticed the poo.

"Yuck," said Bill, and "Poo," said Bert.

"We'll have to send them for cleaning early tomorrow, as we'll need them to dance with the ladies in the evening."

Shocked by their discovery, Hekla whispered with dismay, "They are not really old."

"I think they are up to something. Even their names are different. They are Bill and Bert, not Charles and Ernest," Freya observed.

That night the sheep used their magic to make themselves smaller to hide under the beds. They listened to the naughty men discussing their plan to rob the ladies of their jewellery and money from the safe while the ladies took their morning excursion. The sheep slept well despite Ernest and Charles snoring loudly.

Mavis and Hilda had dreadful headaches in the morning and needed to take some headache pills. As they made their way to breakfast, they had to steady themselves on the handrail that ran along the corridors, and the sea wasn't even rough, just a moderate 4 to 5 on the Beaufort scale with a few crested wavelets. Eventually they made it safely to breakfast, then onto their excursion coach for the beautiful botanical gardens of Madeira.

The naughty men sent their suits for cleaning and took a late breakfast, then returned to their cabin to put their make up and wigs on before leaving again.

The sheep followed the men around the ship. Bert had managed to get a master key for the cabin from the pocket of a careless steward. Disguised, they were soon confidently strolling along the corridor to the ladies' cabin. The sheep followed them and sure enough, they stopped at the cabin door, they looked all around to make sure nobody was watching, and then carefully opened the door. The sheep went in behind the crooks and watched as the pair opened the safe and helped themselves to jewellery and money, which they then stuffed into their casual day jacket pockets. Carefully, the men closed the safe and walked back to their cabin. Once safely inside their cabin, the men put the valuables in a plastic carrier bag that contained their smelly old socks and pants at the bottom of their wardrobe.

Bert rubbed his hands with glee and with a satisfying smile said, "Lovely jubbly." The men removed their make up and wigs and put them back in the drawer once more. Next, they walked to the dining area for a lunch snack. Their snacks were enormous, they piled their plates high with sausage rolls, fish and chips, and spoonfuls of curry sauce. Then went back again to the buffet and loaded up their plates with lots of bits of this and that. Although they were both full up, they still managed to find room for treacle pudding with custard and a couple of profiteroles with cream.

Hekla and Freya knew they had to do something but what? They couldn't let their guard down. So, they put their thinking caps on.

"Lunch will help us think better," said Hekla,

"It will!" agreed Freya and they knew exactly what they were having for lunch. You see after the robbery the sheep had watched the quayside from the deck rails and saw another consignment of hay loaded onto the ship and being taken into the same store room as before.

"So thoughtful of them," Hekla said with a sheepish grin. Freya winked in acknowledgement and soon the mischievous pair managed to get back into the store room and were helping themselves to another tasty lunch. Meanwhile the Head Chef was finishing the evening dinner menu for the 'Royal Gloriana' restaurant which included once again the 'special' of the day - 'lamb smoked in hay' and it was not long before the table reservation list was full.

The ladies returned from their morning trip and changed into their swimwear. This time they wore their one-size fits all cover ups they'd bought that day from the ship's shop which were on special offer. Armed with their sunglasses and sun cream, they took the lift to the sun deck to sunbathe on loungers and were completely oblivious to the fact that they had been robbed. They looked forward to Bingo at 4 pm and to dancing at 8 pm with Ernest and Charles.

At 4 pm the Bingo began. The sheep sat in some unoccupied chairs nearby and watched the goings on in the 'Princess bar' lounge. Bingo didn't come with free nibbles of corn, only a handful of peanuts in a dish on the table, and salted nuts were not good for them. They saw Hilda and Mavis sitting with a whole Bingo book each holding their bright green Bingo dabber pens. Just a short distance away the sheep noticed Hazel, too, was playing Bingo, but alone.

"Maybe we should let Hazel know what's happened, she may help," said Freya.

So, they made their way over to Hazel's table and in a hushed voice Freya said, "It's us."

Hazel immediately leapt up and shrieked "Sheep!"

"That's different, you are supposed to shout 'House' or 'Bingo'," the caller said and everyone laughed. Hazel was embarrassed and said, "Sorry, I made a mistake.

Shortly after Hazel's outburst, the Bingo caller called out "two fat sailors 88" and somebody did say 'House'. It was Hilda. Hilda was so excited as the prize was a whole £125!

After she had calmed down, Hazel whispered, "I know you sheep are here, wherever you are."

The sheep told her about the robbery, and the naughty men. Hazel was speechless. She was concerned though, as she knew that to know about the robbery might implicate her. What to do? She still couldn't believe she was talking to invisible sheep.

When Bingo had finished, Hazel suggested that they all should go somewhere quieter to discuss the robbery. So they all went up to the Observation lounge on Deck

12. There, soft music played so they could chat. To the other passengers Hazel appeared to be talking to herself, but for those who had been at Bingo earlier that afternoon, they thought nothing of it, just that Hazel was a bit odd and probably lonely. Hazel hated their patronising looks.

Then Hekla announced that she had an idea, "Why don't we wait until Hilda and Mavis report the robbery to security. Then, Hazel, you can tell the security officer that you noticed some men acting a bit suspiciously, and had followed them to their cabin and you can point out their cabin."

Hazel thought it was a splendid idea. And so, the sheep showed Hazel where the crooks' cabin was.

Hilda and Mavis were thrilled with the Bingo win and decided to use their winnings towards having their nails manicured and anti-wrinkle face treatments at the on-board beauty spa "Sparkles". They loved being pampered. After their treatment, they complimented each other on their beautiful manicures and radiant looking faces. They returned to their cabin to get ready for the evening. Hilda went to get her jewels from the safe, but when she opened the safe, she froze in horror before letting out a hideous scream, "We've been robbed! Our valuables and jewellery have gone!" Mavis was horrified too, and immediately phoned security.

Meanwhile back in their cabin the crooks were playing cards before readying themselves for the evening. Their suits had been cleaned and returned to their closet, their make-up and wigs were still hidden in the clothes drawer.

The Head of Security Gordon Gashbeard and his assistant Martin arrived at the ladies' cabin carrying their clipboards, pens, and forms. Mavis and Hilda were impressed at his speediness and he introduced himself and Martin. Soon they were all sitting down in the small lounge area of the cabin. Here Gordon took down some details and a description of the missing items and jewellery. The ladies completed a report form and signed it.

"Now, do you have any idea who might be responsible for stealing your valuables?" Gordon asked. They didn't. "Has anyone besides you and your cabin steward been in your cabin?" They told Gordon about Ernest and Charles, "But we're sure they were not responsible, as they were such charming gentlemen," said Mavis. Nevertheless, the ladies gave descriptions of their dancing partners.

Gordon thanked Mavis and Hilda for their help. "We'll do our very best to catch the culprit and get your things back," he reassured them. Shortly afterwards Gordon and his assistant left the ladies' cabin.

The Captain made an announcement on the ship's PA system about the robbery and asked passengers to immediately report anything suspicious that they may have seen to security. Already Gordon and Martin were checking the passenger lists for a Charles and Ernest, but couldn't find anyone matching their names and description.

Hazel and the sheep heard the Captain's announcement as had 'Bill and Bert'. Okay, Hazel knew it was time to act. She phoned security and a short while later Hazel, the sheep, along with Gordon and Martin were making their way to Bill and Bert's cabin. Gordon knocked briskly on the door. Bert answered it. Gordon quickly realised that the pair looked nothing like the description Hilda and Mavis had given him. He was just about to apologise for disturbing them, when suddenly Freya unseen, ran quickly inside and with her teeth and front hoofs opened the make up drawer and pulled out the make-up and grey wigs, which fell to the floor. They all stood and looked on in amazement.

Bert panicked and then with Bill they tried to make a break for it running down the corridor. Gordon's assistant searched the cabin and found the jewellery in the smelly sock bag. Freya and Hekla were, of course, still invisible and in a quick-thinking moment had sprinted out of the cabin and managed to trip the crooks up in the corridor. In next to no time Bert and Bill were flat on their faces and being handcuffed by Gordon. The crooks were marched straight to the ship's brig. (A brig is the name for a ship's prison).

Hilda and Mavis thanked Hazel for her vigilance and Hazel agreed to let the sheep spend the rest of the cruise in her cabin, provided of course they didn't make a mess. Hazel placed a large bath towel on the floor, but of course they didn't need it as they had learned to poo in the loo.

'Lamb smoked in hay' was once more taken off the menu by the very frustrated Head Chef, and was never mentioned again.

What an adventure. Only Hazel knew the truth about the real heroes, the sheep.

Hazel was happy to join Mavis and Hilda that evening, and they happily danced with each other, rather than men. They also decided that, should they go on another cruise, they would leave their expensive jewellery at home and just wear sparkly bling and faux pearls in future. They all enjoyed the rest of the cruise.

As for the sheep they looked forward to telling Malcolm, Bouncer, Mr Boohoo, Geoffrey, and their flock back home on the fells all about their adventure.

Beryl and Farmer Joe and their daughter Jenny had had another lovely holiday in Iceland, and were none the wiser about the Sheep of Poshington Hall Farm's cruise. And, when Hazel was asked how her cruise, went she just smiled and said, "Marvellous."

From afar, in his Troll parlour in the cave under the hill in Iceland, the sheep's friendly Lilts troll had kept a watchful eye on his special sheep friends using his magic. He was glad they'd enjoyed their cruise adventure, but was sure he'd meet them again very soon.